THE ARTIST

JENNA KENT

1

—————

Sean

I never tire of gazing at this painting—it sustained me during the tumultuous storm that followed after my mother's passing. I didn't know it was coming. This anonymous artist, held in high esteem by my mother, holds a heart of gold and extreme talent. She worked for my Mom before cancer took her life, and she shared her art with me every day until the very end.

"You'd love her Sean. She has a heart of gold. But she's also a very sad woman." Those were my mother's last words about her. I wish to God that I knew what she looked like. I'd fall to the floor and ask her to marry me. I don't care what she looks like. This very small catalog of my mother's paintings, I keep close to me. My mother purchased the rights to them for the art gallery on our estate. I've inherited the tech firm that has revived the City of Detroit. Blueprint Enterprises, a firm that specializes in developing social media dating apps. My mother was a talented woman, and very skilled in the art of matchmaking. She's known throughout the city as the

mother of love, and she had very high-profile clientele. With my mother's skillset, my siblings and I entered the tech industry, creating a family empire.

My mother was my everything. She was the reason I am successful today; her belief in me gave me the strength to be who I was. When I told her that I am a lesbian, she already knew and accepted it without question. The only problem is, not everyone else does. My own siblings look at me differently because of how masculine I appear, even though I'm a woman and love women. Being a rich lesbian is difficult as it's hard to find love--now that my mother is gone, I'm not sure if I even want it anymore; to build popular dating apps. Now, we run a billion-dollar company.

I spend most of my days in the office, managing the day to day, and obsessing over the human resource files. I've fucking lost my mind. I'm trying to find this artist by any means necessary. She was on the payroll for the two years she worked at the firm. I've had to have at least brush past her, even if I was buried in writing code. When this beauty worked here, she worked directly under my mother. I was on the lower level, being a fucking slut and working with my siblings to get the framework built for the app. I've narrowed it down to six women. I drop the files on my assistant's desk, grabbing my bike helmet.

"Abby, I expect these women at the dinner party tomorrow night," I announced sternly. "Do whatever is necessary to get them here - even if you have to hand deliver the invites and pay them off with cold hard cash." Abby blushed, fully aware of how determined I was in finding my perfect woman.

I navigated the hallway of cubicles, making my way to the elevators. Down in the parking lot stood my 2022 Ducati sport bike amongst a few other cars I owned. I needed an escape and the speed of my sport bike would provide it. I secured my helmet and revved the engine, soaring off swiftly. Tomorrow marked the anniversary of the passing of my mother, who did so much to build Detroit up again—thus, many wanted to pay homage to her life's work.

I need something to help me relax. I cruise through the city on my bike, down Jefferson Street, skirting the Detroit River. Then I take Jefferson straight to Belle Isle bridge. Once I've reached the Island, I park my bike and walk to the waterfront, inhaling the salty air.

My mind is made up. This woman could be anyone. It doesn't even matter if she's single. I'm going to marry her—whatever it takes. It might sound crazy, but this woman seemed to have captured my essence in a painting. She could see into my very soul.

I remove a photo from my pocket and sit down on the grass, admiring the view of the city from the Island. My gaze falls on the painting that captured my very essence.

It's an image of me, when I was having difficulty appreciating my body. She made me look beautiful. I never truly accepted myself until I observed this painting; one which my mother prominently displayed in her office. She would gaze at it each day and recognize me—the real me.

This woman had to be watching me; she could see me in ways I couldn't even see myself. My mother knew it: she could recognize the gift that this woman has. The thought of her consumes me. Why hadn't my mother introduced us? It must have been because she was married, or something. My mother had connected hundreds of couples, and their relationships were long-lasting. I desired that. I believed my mother knew that this woman was my soulmate, yet I can't understand why she hadn't presented her to me.

But that's alright. I will find her myself. She's out there

somewhere, waiting for me to come and get her. My promise is to give her the world and my heart too. I'll take care of her and she won't have to want for anything.

My phone beeps, pulling me away from my deep musings. I take it out of my pocket, because the only person who has my number is Abby.

"Abby," I say, anxiously awaiting her response. "It's done, Ms. Phillips," she says before I end the call. Just hours between us now; soon enough I will meet the woman made just for me, destined to spend eternity with me.

2

Kara

"Put this dress on," Erica says, passing me a frilly garment. I cringe at the thought of attending the dinner later tonight, but Sean's generous check is too good to pass up. What's so important about her former employees being there? I tug open the package and gape at the length of the dress; it barely grazed my knees. My parents had always been strict in their beliefs, but they'd instilled within me a sense of modesty that refused to allow dresses above my knee-length. Despite my sexuality—and disowned orphan status—I was still attached to certain family traditions. I'm aware that Erica only wants to push me out of my comfort zone, but I can't help but feel hesitant.

My therapist suggested it, and I had to admit that it's a good idea if I want to attract the right woman. The dress was very short and sheer, not something I felt comfortable wearing - but I compromised by pulling on a pair of black leggings to protect my bottom - since the dress ended just below it. It's not easy being a curvy girl with thick thighs, a voluptuous waist, and a round bottom; finding clothes is always a struggle.

I usually keep my long hair braided or pulled up, but this time Erica gives me a makeover. She straightens it and applies light makeup. I still have to wear the bulky glasses; contacts never worked for me - I couldn't stand the application process. Erica examines her work as I stand in the mirror, giving me a thumbs up. Even though she hated that I decided to wear rugged black boots instead of heals, she settled so long as she could get me to the dinner party.

Mrs. Phillips is sorely missed. She was like a second mother to me. It broke my heart when she had to let me go from the company. She said it was too difficult for her, seeing me watch her die. Her generosity and thoughtfulness showed, because the severance she gave me exceeded enough money to cover my expenses for a year. I used some of it to take a much-needed break, but after that ran out, I took on various odd jobs and art projects to make ends meet. I don't care about money or ostentatious possessions; I'm content with just my art. Mrs. Phillips was always so encouraging of my gift--she said I could see people's souls in my pieces. To commemorate her youngest daughter Sean, she commissioned me to draw her.

I became deeply infatuated with Sean. She's stunning. A masculine lesbian with a concerningly large heart. She was brave and fearless but had a cold edge to her. Sean never paid me any mind, no matter how much I stared when she was around. We'd met just after she'd grown into herself and accepted who she was, which quickly attracted women in droves to her door. Why would someone as sought-after as her be interested in settling down? I'm attending the same event as her tonight; she always had such a close relationship with her mother, far better than the rest of the family. Seeing how grief-stricken she was at the funeral made my chest ache. I tried to offer my condolences, but it felt like I was invisible. It'll probably be the same when we meet tonight.

I don't want to attend this dinner; I've moved on from my unhealthy obsession with Sean. I refused to date, hoping she'd notice me, but it never happened. Tomorrow night, a woman from the coffee shop where I work part time has asked me out, and I'm excited. Abby clarified that unless I'm dismissed, I must stay for an hour, or the check won't be honored. Then she offered me $10,000 just to show up with a plus one—enough to pay my rent and utilities for an entire year. I can't turn down this opportunity.

I grab a light jacket. It's the height of summer in Detroit, and the temperature is refreshingly cool. Ideal weather! I reside downtown, already expensive due to gentrification. The dinner is within walking distance, so I only need my keys. I lock up, then stroll with Erica, clutching the ornate invitation needed for entry. The invite reminds me of my mother's fondness for fancy stationery. The dinner is at a high-end bar just down the street from my apartment. We arrive shortly and are welcomed by security. My invitation is accepted; we step inside and are immediately met by servers bearing glasses of champagne.

I spot Sean at the bar, charming a beautiful woman. Nervously, I grab a drink to take my apprehension off the edges. Before I go, I want to say goodbye since I'm moving on. Not that it matters; my fixation with her was just in my imagination. Sean had no clue how I felt about her.

Mortified, I realize looking at her isn't helping. It's reawakening old feelings. She's breathtakingly gorgeous. Her striking green eyes capture the attention of the woman she's with. Sean is huge and muscular, hovering close to seven feet tall. She sports all black clothing--a nice dress shirt and slacks. She has her neck length dark brown hair in a messy bun, loose strands messily fall down her face and neck. Her rosy plump lips make me lick my own. Her arms are more muscular than I remembered from a year ago. She's definitely been working out. Sean tenderly caresses the woman's cheek. Although she doesn't know I'm here, I feel a twinge in my core when I see her.

Because I wish it was me. Her creamy, soft skin makes me want to snuggle under her.

"Damn, she's fine as hell," Erica coos, leering at me. Sean's gaze shifts to the target of our ogling. In a momentary exchange of electric glances, I swear she recognizes me - but her eyes quickly flutter back towards her companion. Embarrassment and heartache hit me anew.

"Come on, let me show you, my painting." I tell Erica. I take her hand and walk her over to the gallery.

3

———

Sean

I had already spoken to five of the former employees, and so far, none of them showed any appreciation for art. I was beginning to lose hope that my "princess" was even at the gallery, but then I noticed the last employee standing in front of the painting I loved the most. Could this be her? With a hesitant heart, I set my drink down on the bar counter and made my way over. They were laughing about something and pointing towards the image, when suddenly everything seemed to stop as soon as I approached them.

What was so funny?

"It's a beautiful piece of artwork. What do you know about it?" I said, trying to contain my frustration. The tall woman with fluffy hair clad in peculiar clothes looked taken aback by my comment. She remained silent, not daring to answer me as she glanced away from me. I then looked towards Kara - the woman that she had referred to earlier - and saw an anxious expression settle in her eyes.

"What do you think of it?" I asked her softly, taking a step closer. She paused before speaking out hesitantly.

"Kara?" I ask with a slight edge to my voice. This woman has worked for my mother before. She's plain, but in her own kind of way, beautiful. Kara's eyes softened as soon as she saw me.

"I like art," she said. "It's a delightful painting."

A scoff escaped from my lips. It was a fucking master-piece. The one painting I loved the most out of my mother's entire collection. Kara swallowed and tucked her long, dark hair behind her ear nervously. I pointed to the DIY painting tables nearby.

"Since you like art so much, Kara, why don't you paint me a picture? Let's see how well you measure up." The venom in my voice was unmistakable. "Or would you rather be dismissed so you can cash your check? I'm sure it will cover your meager wages for a few months-- inflation isn't kind to the poor right now."

The other woman gaped at me as if they were both stunned by my insult. Tears collected in Kara's eyes, but none of them fell; Fuck her tears.

She just insulted my favorite painting. Kara nods and strides to the art table, with the woman in tow.

Fuck it. I'm taking this painting back home. She's not here. I slip my hands into my pockets and trudge back to the bar. My hopes of finding someone special were dissipated; I feel like I'm heartbroken. My gaze keeps returning to Kara, whose hands are smeared with paint as she works at the art table - the only one that even bothered or cared tonight. I had set up the area convinced that my mysterious woman would appreciate it, but instead Kara is merely proving a point; I was rough on her. Hurt people, hurt people.

I down another drink from the bar and wait for everyone

else to leave. Derrica, one of the six, saunters to the bar; we've been friends with benefits before and she has been flirting with me all evening. I start to consider her offer; she can be wild in bed.

"Sean?" someone calls out while I'm still focused on Derrica. I don't bother looking at who it is.

"Your picture," says Kara's voice. "I finished it." Oh, it's her alright...I wave my hand for her to place it on the counter.

"Thanks for coming," I say, not meeting her eyes. She lets out a deep sigh and sets down the small painting. I take a quick glance at her and instantly pause in surprise—she looks so hurt, like I had torn her to shreds. A fleeting pang of guilt washes over me as I remind myself that I'm not such a monster anymore.

I run after her as she turns away with her friend, waving my hands wildly "Wait!" I plead, trying to correct my mistake. She stops and I look softly into her eyes.

"I was awful earlier," I admit regretfully.

"I got defensive when you and your buddy started mocking my mother's painting—my favorite painting—and it was wrong of me. I'm sorry; please understand how much I do appreciate you being here to pay respects."

A tear slides down her cheek and I instinctively brush it away with my thumb. Her friend shoots me daggers of death but I simply raise one corner of my mouth in an amused smirk—it seems she's finding me more attractive than she'd care to admit.

"C'mon Kara, let's go get something to eat," her friend urged as she pulled her away yet again. Kara smiled nervously at me and wiped her tears again before whispering softly.

"I would hug you if it weren't for all the paint on me. I

really loved your mother." My expression softened in response to her sincere words.

"I hope you like the picture." She tells me, then turns away and leaves with her friend.

Derrica is admiring the painting we were just discussing. "Wow, is that the same artist?" she asks, pointing to my favorite painting I so adamantly defended earlier. I grab it from Derrica's hand, inspecting it closely as she leans in.

"It's fantastic isn't it? Definitely has to be the same artist —or maybe she's good at mimicking talent." My heart drops to the floor; my angel was standing right in front of me, and I had shredded her. I drop the painting to the ground and rush for the door, pushing rudely through people to get out to the street. But I'm too late—she's gone.

4

———

Kara

"I don't understand what you see in that asshole!" Erica spat as we stood in Coney Island, just a block away from my apartment. Indulging in some greasy, unhealthy comfort food seemed like the perfect remedy, even if it meant shortening my lifespan by a few years. Sean's ability to shred a person's spirit with her words had caught me off guard once again tonight. I was seething with anger. The hasty painting I had put together depicted her exactly as I saw her—a mean girl, albeit an exquisitely mean girl.

Despite that, Erica was only teasing me about the painting. She knew it was my work and playfully mocked it. I couldn't help but smile, knowing that Sean had taken offense. It was some of my finest work, and her mother had adored that painting so much. I never thought anyone would cherish it after her passing; I had expected it to end up in the trash.

"At least my art still holds up," I said, smiling.

"Damn, that woman is a beast. Sexy, but cruel as hell. She practically called us broke bitches," I chuckled at Erica's remark.

"Can't argue with that," I shrugged.

"Well, don't worry. We won't be seeing her again. The job is done. I'll deposit the check and move on with my life. Did you at least get a phone number?" I asked, knowing Erica had only come along to hunt for potential guys while I paid my respects. She grinned wickedly and held out her phone.

"Three new contacts. Go girl!" I gave her a high five.

After gathering our food, we went our separate ways. Erica lived in a different building just two blocks over. I headed to my rent-controlled apartment, kicked off my shoes, and settled at my small dining table meant for two. I had lived in this apartment for five years, and I couldn't help but wonder how much longer I'd be able to stay. But I loved this place—it's the perfect size for me.

I had ordered chili cheese fries and wing dings, and as I dug my fork into the fries, sulking, a loud knock on the door startled me. My heart raced with nervousness. Was Erica in trouble? Without thinking, I swung the door open, gasping when I saw Sean standing there. How did she know where I lived? Her capacity for cruelty was worse than death itself. Did this mean she wasn't finished with me?

"Kara," her voice came out breathless, as though she had just finished running a marathon. I couldn't bring myself to answer. I was terrified that she was about to make me feel worse than I already did. I slammed the door shut, leaning against it, my body trapped in fear.

"Kara, open the door," she pleaded. I stood there frozen, unable to move. My hands, still covered in paint, hadn't even been washed yet.

"Kara," her voice saying my name caused me to close my

eyes, bracing myself for what would come next. "I will buy your building just to see you. If that's the route you want to take, then fine. I'll leave. But I need to talk to you. And I will." I gasped, turning my body toward the door. I knew her well enough to understand that she meant it. I didn't want her to buy my building. She was on a whole new level of pettiness. I took a deep breath and opened the door.

"May I come in?" she asked, and I let out the breath I had been holding as I heard her words. At this point, I was trembling. Stepping aside, I allowed her to walk into my apartment. She took down her messy bun, smoothing her hair back and re-pinning it. In a rush, I hurried over to my food, covering the lid.

"Coney Island. Good choice for a Friday night," she said with a smile. Was she attempting small talk? With me? I covered my food and hastily stashed it in the fridge. Glancing at my paint-covered hands, I headed to the sink to wash them. Sean slipped her hands into her pockets, surveying my apartment. It was adorned with art tools strewn about and paint bottles. I couldn't claim to be the tidiest person.

"I'm sorry. I wasn't expecting company," I apologized, my eyes darting around as I busied myself with tidying up the tools to create a seating area for her.

"Why didn't you tell me you painted that image?" I froze, meeting her gaze. Why did she even care?

"Well, Sean, you're not exactly the friendliest when you're angry. I couldn't get a word in," I replied, laughter tinged with nervousness escaping me.

"I really messed up," she said.

I shrugged, rushing to my art room to set down the supplies. Then I returned, gesturing for her to take a seat.

"What brings you here? Did I do something wrong?"

Sean looked at me, her stare making me uncomfortable. It was a look I had never seen from her before. Never.

"I never expected you to be so beautiful," I stared at her awkwardly.

"I worked for your mother for two years, Sean. You never even glanced at me. Not once," I stated, observing her as she closed her eyes as if in pain. She took a deep breath, then made her way over to my sofa, sitting down. A moment of silence hung in the air.

"You did nothing wrong, Kara. But to answer your other question: I'm here for you," I gasped, clearly bewildered by her words.

"For me? Is this about the painting?" She sighed, her hungry gaze sweeping over my body, making me feel uneasy. Not just uneasy, but uncomfortably hot. My legs shifted, and my core heated. Sean licked her lips, rising from the sofa. She advanced toward me like a predator closing in on its prey. I instinctively backed away because whatever she had in mind, she was determined to have it. I had no resistance when it came to her. I had desired her for years, ever since I laid eyes on her—a woman finding her way through confusion, transforming into a remarkable individual. I was proud of her. I wanted her.

I loved her.

5

———

Sean

I don't think Kara realizes how heavily she's breathing, practically panting. I yearn to touch her face. The more I look at her, the more memories flood back. She used to be around my mother all the time. I viewed her as a snobbish, unattainable, proper girl. A woman I believed I'd never have a chance with. She always carried her Bible and dressed modestly. This is a far cry from her usual attire. I never paid her much attention because I knew I was gay, and most religious folks can't tolerate that. I still don't know how she would feel about someone like me—a masculine lesbian who defies all the rules. But I'm desperate to find out. She retreats until her back hits the wall of her living room. I trap her, placing my hands on either side of her. She's incredibly beautiful.

"Why did you paint that portrait of me?" I finally ask, a question that has haunted me since my mother's passing. She's panting, clearly nervous because of me, but I can't bring myself to care.

"Your mother asked me to," she breathes out, looking somewhat dizzy. Is she about to faint?

"Is that the only reason?" I press. She saw something in me, something nobody else did. "Kara, please," I plead. She exhales deeply, her gaze lost in the distance as I anxiously await her response.

"I painted that portrait because I loved you," her words cause my heart to race, soaring to a place it has never been before. I've heard those words before, from countless women I've slept with. And I've broken many hearts because I never felt love for anyone.

But now, Kara.

I crush my lips against hers, feeling the love she just confessed in that kiss. Her mouth is so hungry for me, as if she's yearned for this, starving to taste me. It's overwhelming. Her hands hold my face, pulling me deeper into her. I have to tear myself away because I want to claim her right now. I step back, breathing heavily.

"I'm so sorry," she gasps, and I see tears streaming down her face. I rush back to her, pressing her against the wall.

"I'm not sorry, Kara. I wanted that kiss," I say, flashing a playful smile as I use my finger to wipe away her tears.

"You taste like chili cheese fries." She gasps, her hand instinctively covering her mouth. She tries to move away from me, but I don't let her.

"I love chili cheese fries, Kara," I whisper, resting my forehead against hers.

"What's happening? Am I dreaming?" she asks, and I burst into laughter.

"How long have you been waiting for me to show up and be the woman you wanted?" she gasps again.

"Please don't make me," she begs. I pull her into another kiss, and it's just as hungry as the last. Her hands explore my body, conveying her desire for me. Her touches feel inexperienced, as if she's savoring a woman for the first time.

Oh fuck. That turns me on even more.

I pull away once again. She's breathing so heavily that it's alarming. She weakly gasps when my hands move down to her thighs, and I lift her up. She initially struggles with me, likely due to shyness.

"No, stop," she pants. "I'm too heavy."

"Don't be ridiculous. You're fucking perfect," I reassure her. I carry her into the kitchen and place her on the counter. Then, I search for a glass and fill it with cold water. She needs to drink something before she passes out. I raise an eyebrow at her, letting her know I mean business, and she finishes the glass. It takes a minute for her to calm down, but I'm patient. I've been waiting for a woman like her my whole life.

"You loved Kara? Past tense?" She exhales heavily.

"I got tired of waiting, Sean. I'm ready to move on," she responds. I frown at her answer.

Hell fuck no, she's not moving on. She's mine.

I growl at her, and she stiffens.

"No, Kara. I'm here now. And I'm not leaving," I assert. She lets her head hit the wall of the counter. I slide over to the fridge and retrieve the food she bought.

"Here, eat. This stuff isn't good a day later. I'm sure you know that," I say. She shakes her head, and my frustration grows.

"I'm trying not to fuck you into submission, Kara. Eat. Your. Food," I command. She opens the plate in front of her and grabs the fork, plunging it into her chili cheese fries. Kara takes a bite right in front of me. She's so submissive. Damn, another plus. I enjoy dominating my women, but it often becomes overwhelming for anyone I'm dating. With

Kara, it's as if she yearns for me to dominate her. I swallow, feeling myself losing control. Jesus.

I take the fork from her and have some fries, then I lean in to kiss her. She accepts me willingly, as if my mouth belongs to her.

"Now we both taste like chili cheese fries," I remark, finally coaxing a smile out of her. I rub her thighs, watching her eat. Even this simple act turns me on. I'm ridiculously turned on right now. After she finishes her food, I refill her glass with cold water. Sure, it's not the best beverage for this greasy meal, but I just want to make sure her belly is full. We gaze at each other for a long moment, both of us lost in the moment.

"Have you ever been with a woman, Kara?" I ask. She shakes her head, and her face falls. She's immediately sad again. I fucking hate seeing that expression on her.

"What's wrong, Kara?" I cup her face, forcing her to meet my eyes.

"I'm scared," she quickly responds. She's afraid, but I need clarification on what exactly she's afraid of.

"What are you afraid of, Kara?"

"You. You're going to break my heart," she confesses. I let out a sigh of relief. I was terrified for a moment, thinking she was going to tell me she was confused about her sexuality. But she's only afraid that I'm going to hurt her. She doesn't understand. I need her more than I need air right now.

6

———

Kara

It's like a dream, being with Sean right now. She's doing all the right things, everything I have yearned for. But it feels too good to be true. I can't help but doubt its reality. Sean pulls me closer, her lips grazing my forehead, and I let out another breath, my nerves still trembling with fear.

"Have you ever been with a woman, Kara?" Sean asks once again, bringing up the complicated questions. I can't lie to her. I shake my head, my voice barely above a whisper. "No."

Sean sighs, a mixture of understanding and frustration. "Kara, I never gave you the time of day because you appeared to be a straight woman. I misread the signals. Seeing you dressed modestly and carrying your Bible around, plus coming to terms that I was a gay woman, I couldn't comprehend my growing desire for you." I look away from her when I hear her words, but she cups my face, forcing me to meet her gaze.

"Eventually, I realized I was gay. I came out to my family a few years ago, and my siblings rejected me. My mother understood, but it wasn't enough at the time." She explains.

My heart aches for her, realizing the struggles she has faced. I let out a heavy sigh and respond, "I started carrying the Bible around to try and suppress my yearning for you. I wanted you so badly, but I couldn't make sense of it. And when I finally came out, just before your mother laid me off, I had no one and nothing. Erica has been a good friend, she's straight. But these past couple of years have been lonely. Tomorrow, I have a date with a nice girl I met at the coffee shop who has shown interest in me." I didn't mean to let that slip out, but it did. I feel comfortable being honest with Sean. Besides, she's known for dating multiple women. I know I'm just one of many.

Sean growls, her frustration evident. "A date? Kara, you're not single anymore. You're officially off the market."

I gape at her, taken aback by her possessiveness. "What?" I manage to say, my mind trying to comprehend what she's saying.

Her hand gently strokes my cheek, a mix of tenderness and determination in her eyes.

"It's late, and I'd feel better knowing you've gotten some sleep. We'll talk about this tomorrow." Sean picks me up effortlessly, carrying me down the hall in search of my room. She pauses for a moment when she notices my art room but quickly resumes her task, kicking open my bedroom door and placing me on the bed.

"I'm not canceling my date," I protest, determined to assert my independence. There's no way I can let go of an opportunity for companionship. But Sean growls again, this time more fiercely.

"Yes, you are. You're not a single woman anymore, Kara. You're mine," she asserts, her possessiveness taking hold.

I gape at her, feeling a mix of conflicting emotions. She kneels down, her gaze locking with mine, and I bite my lip nervously. Her commanding presence is both intimidating and enticing, and a part of me longs to obey her, to give her whatever she wants. But deep down, I fear that giving in to her completely will lead to heartbreak. I've never seen her be exclusive with anyone before.

"No. You'll break my heart. I've already told you I love you. Please, just let a love-sick girl go," I plead, my voice laced with vulnerability.

"NO," Sean growls firmly, her tone leaving no room for negotiation. Then, without hesitation, she removes her clothes, leaving herself in a sports bra and boxers.

"Take off your clothes, Kara. Let's go to bed and talk about this in the morning," she commands, her voice carrying a mixture of desire and determination."Come on, Kara," Sean beckons, reaching out to pull me into her warm embrace.

"So that's it? I'm your girlfriend, and you're staying over?" she chuckles, her voice filled with delight.

"You're obviously new to this. You don't know how lesbians behave when they fall in love," she continues, and I can't help but feel a surge of hope. Was that her way of telling me she loves me? Snuggling into her arms, I find myself drifting off to sleep quickly, feeling safe and content.

The next morning, I wake up to the sound of the shower running, steam wafting into the bedroom from the master bathroom. Sean walks out, clad in fresh underwear with a towel draped over her neck. Her hair is still damp from a recent wash. Sitting up on the bed, I rub my eyes, trying to process the reality of the situation. So, it wasn't a dream.

She has an electric toothbrush in her mouth, her eyes fixed on me as she dries her hair. Removing the toothbrush, she turns it off and greets me with a warm smile. Then she disappears back into the bathroom to rinse and gargle. I watch her, puzzled about how she managed to have a toothbrush here. When she emerges from the bathroom once again, I stand up, feeling a bit self-conscious. I'm plagued by Coney Island morning breath, the worst kind. Sean follows me into the bathroom, observing me as I grab my toothbrush.

"I had Abby stop by and bring me some fresh clothing, along with delivering one of my cars. Since you're stubborn about a date, I'm taking you out for the day," she announces, her words catching me off guard as I brush my teeth. A date? I gape at her, toothbrush still in my mouth.

She smiles and turns to her neatly arranged clothes on the bed. "I took the liberty of canceling your date for you," she adds casually. I gasp, feeling a mix of shock and disbelief. She holds up my phone, revealing that she has taken matters into her own hands. My date has received a photo of me in bed with Sean. I can't find the words to respond to that, so I say nothing. I toss my phone back onto the bed and retreat back into the bathroom, closing the door behind me to finish brushing my teeth.

After rinsing, I turn on the shower, grateful that the water is still hot. I let the water cascade over my head, enjoying the sensation. As the shower comes to an end, I wrap myself in a towel and step out of the bathroom. Sean is sitting on the bed, fully dressed and looking effortlessly lovely. Her damp, tousled hair is brushed back, stopping at the nape of her neck. She's wearing a simple t-shirt and sweatpants, and her socks are so pristine white that they could be fresh out of the packaging. Of course, she's a billionaire; she can afford a new pair of socks every day for the rest of her life.

I try to walk past her quickly, but Sean is always two steps ahead. She anticipates my intention to escape and catches me, pulling me into her lap. "I'd like my morning kiss now," she declares with a wide smile, her eyes sparkling with affection.

7

———————

Sean

Based on Kara's expression, I don't think she caught the part about me being a creature of chaos. She has already become my wife to me. I just need to get to know her better - her favorite colors, foods, and of course, her painting style. She'll be painting a lot in our new home. She gives in because I would have taken it anyway. Her lips are sweet against mine and full of love; I'd like nothing more than to stay here in bed with this angel all day, but I do the right thing instead and take her out. She doesn't understand how much she means to me.

She changed my life without knowing that she was doing it. I was alone and in darkness before she came into my world; I didn't think anyone could relate to what I was feeling. But Kara saw.

I deepen the kiss, wanting to absorb every moment before reluctantly breaking away.

"Get dressed. I'm taking you out." She nods and rises from my lap, walking to her dresser. I'd already gone through her underwear and sniffed them like a creep—desperate to know the smell of her sex. No matter how much they were washed, her scent lingered.

Kara pulls on her panties, sliding them up her legs. I lick my lips, desperate for a peek at her pretty pussy. With effort, I stand and leave the room, knowing that if I got a glimpse, I'd be eating her pussy within seconds. It was untasted and untouched—just waiting to be claimed by me. My mouth would be the only mouth it ever knew.

My attention shifts to the art room, admiring Kara's current works in progress. She was a beautiful artist and I couldn't wait to show her the studio I'd built in our apartment—our future home.

Eventually she steps out of the bedroom, fully dressed. Her damp wavy hair is braided over one shoulder; while she wears a long slender dress which falls gracefully to her ankles, plus flip flops for footwear. She walks into her own studio.

"Where are you taking me?" She leans beside me as my eyes focus on an unfinished painting of a whale in the ocean. The details in her work mesmerize me every time.

"Do you like it?" She asks me. Yes, I freaking love it. I swivel and meet her gaze, pleased she changed out of that tight dress. I love that she looks unapproachable.

Because she is.

I stretch my hand to her face and caress her cheek. She adjusts her bulky glasses which I'm planning on misting up while we're making love. I can't help myself; I lean in to kiss her, desperate for the taste of her lips again. I won't be content until she's at home in my bed as a permanent tenant.

"Where would you like me to take you? I don't know what you enjoy, so you'll have to teach me." I'll do whatever she desires except leave her alone. If she wants to go shopping, I'll take her shopping. I just want to spend time with Kara and learn more about her. She runs her fingers down the sides of her gown, flattening it out. My mouth waters from my ravenous stare. She's gorgeous. Kara flushes from my lusty look.

"Take me to the park." She says, shrugging. I narrow my eyes at her. A park? Of course, she'd choose the least expensive option. From my experience, the first thing a woman wants to do is try to deplete my pockets.

"Okay." I say, retrieving my keys from my pocket. She grabs a jacket together with her purse and keys and follows me out of her apartment, locking the door behind her. She's not coming back here anytime soon. Now that I have her, I'm bringing her home with me.

My truck idles outside the building, unblemished by so much as a parking ticket; the city workers know my plates. I start the engine and open the passenger door for her, helping her climb in. She's quiet on the drive, glancing at me occasionally as we cruise down Jefferson Ave. I take her hand in mine, comforting her yet also letting myself be comforted. I wish I had thought to grab food--I can take care of that later though. I want to talk to her, ask questions, learn more about her and when she realized she was in love with me.

Finally, I pull up to Belle Isle, one of my favorite spots in Detroit. Even though she must have visited before, being a native Detroiter, there's something special here for us; it's where I fell in love with her. We walk over to a bench facing the river, and she hops up and swings her pretty legs while watching the water flow past.

"I come here often," I tell her. "When my mother passed away, this spot kept me going." Then I dig out the photo from my pocket and hand it over to her; its edges are worn and crinkled from overuse. I ought to get another copy printed, but somehow I'm attached to this one.

"And you, Kara. This image showed me I wasn't all alone; someone else understood what I was feeling. You, Kara. You witnessed me at my worst. When no one else wanted to listen, except for my mom." She inhales sharply, her eyes fixed on the photo.

8

Kara

I run my hand across my forehead, gazing at the photo of my painting. I recall Sean's mother requesting me to paint her. She wanted me to catch the essence of what Sean was going through. So, I spent days clandestinely shadowing Sean and her moods. What's more, as I did this, I was falling head over heels for her. I wanted to be one of many women she had gone through.

I take a deep breath and brush my hand over the crinkled photograph. She has surely looked at it countless times.

"Your mom wanted a portrait of you; one that captured your true soul. She confided in me that you were her special child. Her favorite." I offer a playful wink at Sean. Here comes the hard part; so, I take a deep breath before speaking again.

"I couldn't get you to say more than two words to me whenever I made attempts to talk with you. That is why I followed you." My eyes remain glued on the image, recollecting Sean's anguish; yet, I was powerless to do anything about it. All she thought of me was that I was some bible thumping moralist.

"The night I watched you fight with your siblings, I painted the image. You came out, and they rejected you; I captured your pain, the rejection you felt, and the new you crawling out of the former shell of yourself. And I loved you that night. Nobody else ever had my affections as you did."

My throat constricted at the thought, suppressing tears. As I stared at the beautiful river, lost in thought of that night when I painted the image, I hadn't noticed Sean wrap her arms around my waist and pulling me into her lap.

"I love you, Kara." My breath caught at her words and I looked into Sean's tear-stained eyes. Before I could utter a word, she pressed her lips to mine. In that moment, all sound had faded away and waves of love enveloped me— one that had been building for what felt like an eternity. With increasing passion, she explored me with her hands and mouth—devouring every inch of my flesh which seemed to be a proclamation of sorts.

"Sean," I whispered amidst a ragged breath between kisses. When Sean bit down on my neck as if claiming me, my eyes rolled back in ecstasy. Gripping onto my arms firmly as if restraining herself, she growled before releasing me just enough so we could look each other in the eye— both breathing heavily.

"First, I'm feeding you Kara. Then, I'll take you home." I nervously nod and she pulls me off her lap. She holds my arm in a tight grip, tugging me to her truck. Then she lifts me up like I'm light as air, almost throwing me in the passenger side of the vehicle. She slams the door and hastily jumps in the driver's seat. Sean starts the engine and takes us off the Island. She stays silent for a while as she steers us back into Downtown Detroit.

"Do you want something to eat?" She inquires, turning toward Greek Town. Can't go wrong here - there are too many restaurants to count. I shrug.

"Whatever you want." I tell her; but when she looks at me, I regret my statement. While we wait at the stoplight, she bites her lip, gazing at my legs.

"Okay, pizza." I say hurriedly, hoping to bring her concentration back on track. Sean turns her eyes back to the road and stops in front of an upscale pizza place. Uh oh, this isn't what I had in mind; spending fifty bucks on a single large is too much for me.

"I think less pricey--" Her glare makes me pause.

"You are in my possession, Kara," she snaps. I sigh and decide to let it go. The valet helps me out of the truck as Sean takes my hand and pulls me into the restaurant.

The hostess notices Sean and gives her five-star treatment. We skip the line and are taken up the stairs to a private dining area reserved for high-profile guests. Sean pulls out a chair for me before sitting down, and I blush at her gentlemanly gesture.

"Just a pepperoni pizza is fine," I say, not bothering to look at the menu. Sean slides her seat closer to me and holds my chin as she pulls me into a deep kiss. "I miss your lips already," she murmurs between kisses.

The hostess arrives and orders for us: a simple pepperoni pizza and two sodas. As we wait, Sean holds my hand and occasionally plants gentle kisses on it while I glance around the restaurant.

"Sean, what now?" I ask her when the moment is right. We've already declared our love for each other – what's the next step? She smiles at me, proud and excited, before answering, "Well since you asked, my plan was to bring you back home to my place and get you settled in." My jaw drops open in disbelief; she's acting like I agreed to move in with her instantly. *Take it down a notch, killer!* We've spent just one night together and that was against my will.

"Sean, I can't just move in with you," I said sternly. She stared back at me with those same bright eyes, her cheeks still rosy from the warmth of our passionate declaration.

"Yes, you are, Kara," she insisted, as if nothing I had said had an impact. "I told you earlier.... You are a kept woman now. I'm keeping you."

The fuck?! No way! Even though I don't typically curse, my goodness this woman was downright absurd. Taking a sip of my drink, I scrambled to wrap my head around how I might get out of this — but the real question is, did I even want to?

9

Sean

I'm on a love high, and it feels amazing. My sweetheart gazes at me with her mouth wide open. Yes, she'll be joining me in my place tonight. I've been eagerly awaiting this moment for an eternity. Kara's the beauty who always stood by my mom's side. At first I was envious of that relationship, thinking my mother wanted to replace me with a goody two shoes bible princess. But I soon realized that wasn't true—my mom held Kara close because she knew this woman was meant for me.

It's crazy, but I finally have all my ducks in a row. Nothing can keep me away from Kara now. When I told her I loved her, something I've never said to anyone before, it felt real and eternal. She's the start of a whole new story in my life.

"You're insane," Kara says. Far from being offended, I'm actually flattered by the comment. My next move is to show her just how serious I am—I plan to ravish her in bed until she agrees to take my last name by the end of the week. My methods might be calculated and unorthodox, but this woman? She's mine until my last breath. Just then, the hostess arrives with the pizza, and I offer Kara a slice.

I will take care of her, for the rest of her life. She bites hungrily into her slice, closing her eyes to savor its flavor.

"Kara, why didn't you sign your painting? I thought it was customary for artists to sign their work." She looks up at me with her mouth still full. I smile at her. As she chews and swallows, I quickly place another slice on her plate.

"I don't know," she answers finally. "I never sign my paintings. I'm not much of a people person, and I don't like too much attention over my work. I just enjoy painting." Finished with her slice, she stares up at me again. The musty scent of pizza in the air fills my nose as I gaze upon her beauty; I silently chastise myself for not feeding her first.

"Aren't you eating?" She reaches over and grabs a slice, placing it on my plate before I can answer. If she wants to get technical with that question, then she needs to hurry and finish eating so I can take her home—because the only thing I want to eat right now is her, and I'm willing to go on a fast until I get what I want.

I meet her gaze steadily and reply calmly:

"I'm not hungry."

"How? You haven't eaten anything all day. You don't like pizza?" She watches intently as my eyes drop down to her lap, my mouth watering in anticipation of the treat that awaits there. With a sigh, she sets down her pizza slice and leans in closer to me.

"I love pizza," I whisper faintly "But I'm interested in something else right now."

"Me? You want to eat me?" I exhale, not saying a word.

Yes, yes I do. To have you laid out on the table with your legs spread - that's the only course I'm anticipating. Pizza can wait.

Kara does something unexpected next; she grabs my hand and hikes up her dress. We are alone in this room. The waitress occasionally pops by to check on us. She takes my hand and positions it on her exposed thigh.

"I've never done this before," she whispers, removing my hand but she quickly wraps her fingers around mine, repositioning it back onto her lap.

She looks around for a moment then back at me.

"It's okay. I want to feel this." Is she trying to undermine the little authority I have left? Every passing minute astounds me more and more. Or perhaps, she is just as famished for me as I am for her. Her leg parts for me and she reclines into her seat, letting me savor a morsel of what's to come.

"If you get a sample of what you desire, will you eat then?" My mouth curves into a smirk at her effort to care for me. I inch closer towards her, pressing my lips against her pizza-stained ones.

"I'll do whatever you want Kara," I murmur softly in her ear before drawing back to gaze into her eyes. She swallows hard and releases an unsteady breath before stretching out her legs invitingly for me.

"Touch me." She whispered, her legs parted and her wetness glistening in the dim light. I slid my hand between her thick thighs, my mouth watering at the sight of her dampness. She moaned quietly as I slipped my fingers under her silk blue panties. Her body had been begging for me to touch her there. In a moment of anticipation, I pressed against her swollen nub, teasing her with pleasure.

"Oh," she breathed out. Her small hands fell onto my wrist, gripping it tightly- not wanting me to stop but pushing my hand further into her warmth. Her face turned away from mine as she closed her eyes, panting. I couldn't help but moan when she ground into my fingers. My sweetheart needed to get off. I pulled Kara into another deep kiss, taking in her moans while I rubbed against the swollen clit until she finally exploded with screams of pleasure that echoed through the room. Her panties were completely drenched along with my fingertips and she continued to quiver as the orgasm slammed into her body. Uncontrollable movements followed and her leg lifted up into the seat spreading wider for me.

I gripped her face firmly, making sure that our eyes met each other's gaze before I murmured "Look at me Kara," while caressing her cheek with my thumb.

"Take a deep breath, baby." Kara panted as she complied with my command. I inserted two fingers into her wetness, eliciting a gasp from her and a wince of discomfort. She was so tight. I quickly removed my fingers and sighed in relief. Then I slid them into my mouth to savor her taste. It was like a drug—tantalizingly sweet, just like candy on my tongue.

Withdrawing my fingers from my mouth, I reclined in the chair and shut my eyes, savoring the flavor of her essence. But then a squeal disrupted me. As I opened my eyes, Kara was readjusting her dress, evidently startled by someone—the waitress who stood before us.

"I'm sorry to interrupt, but can I get you anything else?" The server stammered over her words; it was clear that she was aroused by the scene.

"Just the check and a to-go box," I replied with amusement at the flicker of disappointment passing over her face. If Kara asked me to, I'd call this woman for a three-some—but only if Kara wanted it too. Right now, my attention was solely on her. Even if she was interested in another person joining us, it wasn't an option.

Kara

Did I just lose my virginity in this restaurant? Embarrassment should have settled in, considering I had just gotten caught getting fingered by Sean at the table. But instead of shame, I wanted more.

The waitress leaned in front of me to grab my finished plate, her eyes hungrily lingering on mine. When Sean placed her hand over my chest possessively, the waitress almost growled as if she was claiming me from her.

"Down girl, this one is off the market." Sean growls.

"Too bad," the waitress purred, biting her lip suggestively.

"I'm open to being a third." Although tempting, I politely declined with a knowing smile—perhaps even tinged with a bit of pride at Sean's jealousy.

"No thank you for the offer, but I'm not open to sharing," I said before she could push further. The waitress nodded before walking away with the check.

"The nerve!" Sean scoffed when she left. This wasn't the

first time someone had pursued me like that—unless Julia counted. It seemed like every day for months she would come into the coffee shop where I worked until one day during closing she mustered up enough courage to ask me out after complimenting a female celebrity.

I glanced down at my modest dress and wondered if maybe if I changed up my look, more women would take interest in me? Sean growled again as if guessing what I was thinking.

"Mine." She says to me. I can't fight the smile that forms across my face—I want this, I want her to claim me. I nod and straighten my face into a grin as the waitress returns with our pizza and a check. Sean is quick to pay, placing her credit card on the bill along with some cash for the tip. The waitress comes back with a receipt for Sean to sign before quickly boxing up our pizza.

She grabs my hand and practically drags me away from the table in a rush. "We're going home, NOW." She growls. I can only laugh in response. We move so fast that even the valet has her truck ready when we arrive at the door.

"Let's go back to my place," I suggest, "I'll pack some clothes..."

But she just smiles in that same smug way as before. "You already have clothes where we're going. My home is your home now."

I gasp incredulously. "You don't even know my size. You just met me..."

Sean stops at a light and looks over at me with a sly glint in her eye. "While you were sleeping, I gave Abby some of your clothing sizes so she could build a wardrobe at my apartment." Now it's my turn to be smug—she knew exactly what she was doing all along. We drive off together, holding each other in the darkness.

"Oh my god, you're insane." She leaned in to kiss me, and I didn't reject her—there was a perverse part of me that enjoyed the feeling of her obsessing over me. That could mean something is wrong with me. I allowed her to take me to her loft, which was located in a high-rise apartment building near the riverfront.

Sean pulled me into the luxurious lobby, where there was a lounge area and recreation center. "Wow," I murmured as she dragged me through it. We arrived at an elevator with a keypad; she entered a code and the doors opened.

"This is just temporary, Kara, you'll stay here with me until we find a house."

I hesitantly followed her into the elevator as she mentioned something about a house. It jerked upward and opened to Sean's apartment. The sprawling space had a distinct bachelorette vibe, complete with a kitchen bar. Sean deposited the pizza box on the counter, kicked off her shoes, and peeled off her shirt revealing a toned physique beneath her sports bra and sweats. I couldn't help but admire her chiseled chest and abs. She sauntered towards the bedroom, and I trailed behind like a dog sniffing for scraps.

The bedroom was luxurious–a king-sized bed with an ottoman attached at the end, an enormous TV mounted on the wall, and a headboard made of pure oak covered in pillows. There were several matching dressers sprawled around the room, one long dresser sitting just under the televisions, and a large fish tank with special lighting and lots of wood and leaves sitting atop another dresser. My curiosity got the best of me as I walked over to peer inside. Was it some exotic fish? A lizard? A snake? I couldn't see anything until I noticed a hole in the covering.

"What was supposed to be here?" I asked Sean as she

rummaged through her walk-in closet. She re-emerged with a little black night gown in hand.

Sean sauntered over to my side to inspect the barren tank before resuming her hunt for clothing.

"Damn, Charlotte escaped again. I was supposed to feed her yesterday. Routines are important for them and if you miss, they get anxious." She mumbled, setting clothing down on the bed and scouring the apartment.

Escape? What's escaped the tank? I followed Sean out of the room, my gaze transfixed on her as she surveyed each corner of the place.

"She never goes too far. She must be in here somewhere."

"Sean, what got out?" She didn't respond; instead heading towards the sofa and yanking off its cushions.

"She loves dark places."

"Oh." I moved towards the counter with a pizza box atop it which shifted slightly under my weight like something was pushing at it from inside. Trembling, I lifted it off -just to drop it to the ground in horror when what stood before me became clear. A large, hairy tarantula slowly advanced across the marble surface, much bigger than my hand in size with its fur-covered body. Fear locked me into place and I couldn't move nor scream. The spider took another step forward and paused, its many eyes boring into me. My breaths came quicker and shorter -they said spiders could detect fear after all so perhaps it had sensed mine through thin air. Abruptly it raised its legs up and exposed two menacing fangs that petrified me even further.

"Charlotte! Be nice to your mother!" Sean chastised it sharply. Mother? She wasn't its mother by any stretch of imagination! I could feel my heart thundering in my chest and saw stars in front of my eyes while Sean effortlessly captured Charlotte with a capturing device before moving over and presenting me with a clear container where she now sat walled in -that's how familiar she seemed with this situation. The world spun around me before everything faded to blackness.

"She's harmless, baby." Those words were the only thing I heard before my legs gave out and all I could see was Sean rushing towards me to catch me as I fell. She gently places the container on the counter and stops me from falling completely. Barely conscious, I felt her arms under my legs as she lifted me up and cradled me in her arms.

"Baby?" She asked with a hint of concern in her voice as I completely faded away into darkness.

"Alright, no spiders," Sean muttered, carrying me out of the room.

11

Sean

I call Abby right away after I put Kara to bed. She arrives soon, scowling when she sees what I asked her to pick up.

"Take it to the pet shop in Garden City—I've already sent them cash via PayPal." Abby grimaces but takes the container with Charlotte inside.

"I want a raise." Of course she does, and she will get one.

"We can talk terms in the morning." She covers the container with a towel and leaves. Though I'm sorry to let Charlotte go, I'd choose Kara over anything else. After changing her out of her dress into a gown, I lie by her side on the bed, watching TV while she sleeps. Watching her rest brings me peace, yet I worry about her—I feel like an idiot for bringing her here without getting to know her better. I should have gotten rid of Charlotte earlier.

Kara stirs and turns towards me. Reaching out, I stroke her cheek, pushing back loose strands from her braid. But she must think it's a spider and slaps my hand away, then sits up in terror, looking around. Before she has time to react further, I jump over and pin her down on the bed—wrist restrained above her head. Her tears break my heart.

"I want to go home," she sobs. My heart breaks at her words.

"You are home, sweetheart. I'm so sorry. She's gone, Charlotte is gone." But my words do nothing to console her. She thrashes against my grip and continues to cry. I don't know what to do; she needs something to calm her down. Desperately, I press my lips onto hers, kissing her fiercely. It takes a moment, but eventually her body gives in to me. She kisses me back hungrily and Charlotte fades into the background. I let go of her wrists, allowing my hands to explore her body as I deepen our kiss. She moans and moves against me, wrapping her arms about my neck. It feels amazing to have her in my bed like this. My hands leave her lips and travel down to her breasts; I pull them out of the gown and take one of them into my mouth, suckling it eagerly.

"Sean," she breathes out my name and I know exactly what she needs from me. Her hands cling to my hair as I move lower on her body, lifting up the gown that I was too hasty in putting on earlier - now regretting it deeply – wanting her naked instead. Her legs part for me and I slide my fingers over the sides of her panties before pulling them down. I ache to taste her sweet pussy; positioning my face against it, I pause to admire how beautiful her pink pussy is – wet with desire and hot with arousal. My mouth waters and I lick my lips before diving in. She lets out a scream when she feels my tongue sweep up and down the folds of her center. With two fingers, I spread open her entrance further before pushing deep into her with my tongue.

"Sean, Ahhhh!" She cries out in pleasure. Her hands grip the sheets tightly, thrashing her head from side to side. Her body involuntarily shifts as I pull her back against my mouth. I can't get enough of her taste. My hands move to her thick thighs and tug them closer to me. She's shaking, fighting my every move while I send her into a frenzy. I take a hand to her chest, squeezing and teasing her nipples as I drive my tongue deep into her sex. Her climax hits hard, nearly crippling her with its intensity. She screams and writhes beneath me, gripping the sheets until it almost feels like she'll tear them apart. Even as she begs me to stop, I don't let go - not before I've taken every ounce of pleasure that's leaking from her. I eagerly lick and suck even more, relishing in the deliciousness.

"One more, Kara." I can see her struggling to keep up with me. I take two fingers and plunge them into her depths as my teeth drag across her clit. She screams out in pleasure, trying to hold back the orgasm that's about to take over. Her body trembles from the wave that crashes against her. Feeling her pussy grip my fingers tightly, it turns me on even more than before. I want to lick and savor every inch of her all night long. Her hands weakly pull at my neck, but I don't yield. Leaning away from her lips, I start to kiss and suckle each of her nipples, taking in their sweetness as my fingers swirl in and out of her.

"You're gonna kill me!" she cries out. With my face between her breasts, laughter escapes me. That seems to be a special spot for her; the moment my tongue touches her nipple again, she breaks apart screaming with pleasure as she reaches her third climax. I want yet another one out of her but I restrain myself, knowing it might push her over the edge. We've already had enough sex to knock someone out cold. Moving my head to meet hers, I give her a sweet kiss on the lips before pulling away completely when she's too delirious for words. Rolling off of her, I grab a thin blanket and wrap it around our bodies as I hold her close until sleep comes for us both.

12

———————

Kara

That was incredible. I awoke to the blazing sunlight streaming in from Sean's bedroom window. She was watching me, softly caressing my face.

"Do you feel safe now? She's gone. No more spiders." Sean soothed me. Her messy morning hair fell over her face, making her even more beautiful. With her arm propped up on the bed, she gently stroked my cheek and smiled.

"Spiders?" I was still dazed from the experience. My body ached from wonderful love-making - an ache that I wanted to feel again. Sean chuckled and leaned in to kiss me.

"I want more of you Kara, but I was rough with you last night. I was desperate to calm you down. You need to soak." I roll onto my back, staring up at the ceiling. The sheets slipped down my chest, exposing my bare breasts. Sean's eyes followed them, and she licked her lips, biting her lip as if she were trying to resist attacking me again. Sean thought she had been rough last night, but I thought it had been incredible. She drove me to three orgasms. She kissed me, touched me in ways I had dreamed of experiencing. I also loved that my body drove her wild; she couldn't help herself. Her mouth was on my breasts before I looked back at her. It was my hot spot—the one place that you could touch to instantly get me ready for sex. Her hands gripped my breasts, pulling them together. She buried her mouth over my nipples, devouring them. My mouth parted, and my head fell back from the sensation. I was startled when an alarm went off, though I couldn't place where it was coming from. Sean groaned, biting my nipples once more, sending me to a place between hell and bliss before she let go of me. She rolled off the bed, smoothing her disheveled hair behind her neck. She opened the drawer at the end table beside the bed, pulling out a smart phone.

"Yeah?" She answered brusquely. She groaned again, running her fingers through her hair, clearly annoyed by whoever was on the phone.

"Alright. I'll be there in fifteen minutes." She hung up the phone and tossed it back into the drawer.

"Fuck," she hisses, hands on her hips. I sit up and cover my breasts, watching her silently as she mulls over what to do. Our eyes meet. She sighs before climbing into the bed with me.

"I have to go into the office-- there's been a DDOS attack on our servers and it'll take all day to fix it." She takes my hand in hers and presses it to her lips tenderly.

"Okay, you can take me home on the way," I say, attempting to get out of bed. She stops me abruptly though, pushing me back onto the mattress and pinning my wrists down.

"No Kara, I want you to stay here-- wait for me until I

return." My eyes widen at the thought of staying put for the whole day.

"All day? No... I should go home." Her grip tightens around my wrists as she speaks again.

"I know you'd get bored at the office and besides, this is now your home too." I'm quiet for a moment before speaking up again.

"Okay," I reply softly. "A relaxation day then?" A beautiful smile appears on her face before she leans forward to kiss me passionately.

"I love you so much Kara," she whispers against my lips.

"I love you too," I tell her. She jumps off me and hurries to the bathroom. I can hear the toothbrush whirring then the shower running. I sit up on the bed and my hand falls on my aching core—wow, I am sore. Memories of my sister's wedding night come back to me; it was different with a woman though. Maybe not. Penetration is penetration. I wish I could call her to ask for aftercare tips, but that would break biblical law. My family won't acknowledge me anymore; they've told everyone that I'm dead—the cruelest thing one can do to their own child. But my parents follow God's laws.

Sean's shower is quick; she looks beautiful in nothing but a towel as she skips out of the bathroom, drying her damp curls with another one. She walks over to the dresser and pulls out her underwear; this is the first time I've seen her naked. My mind goes straight to the gutter as she slips into her boxers; when she catches me gawking at her plump behind, she tosses a wet towel from her face right at my head.

"Get your mind out of the gutter, sexy girl." She teases me, and I want to play back so much. She dons a sports bra beneath her clean t-shirt and comfortable sweatpants then moves back to the bed.

"I'm going to send Abby over for aftercare." I wince at the thought of the assistant who had my underwear...She strokes my cheek tenderly.

"This may take all day. There's cash on the counter so you can order food. The doorman will make sure it's delivered. You can explore the apartment; just don't leave, please? I don't want to come home to an empty apartment." I nod nervously, biting my lip. She pulls me in for an intimate kiss on my forehead, slips on a pair of sneakers, and leaves. I feel hollow when I hear the elevator doors close.

13

Kara

After a long, luxurious soak in the bathtub, I force myself to get out. Toweling off, I cast my eyes around the closet for something to wear. My clothes were in the hamper near the front door; I'd find the laundry room later. Amongst several shopping bags on the floor of her closet, I stumble upon fancy underwear that matches my size. Pulling on the bra and panties, I rummage through the other bags and grab a nice short dress and leggings - it reminds me of what I had borrowed for the dinner party the other night. After dressing, I take a brush from the bathroom and comb my damp hair into a braid. As soon as I do it, though, I stop abruptly. I'm used to keeping my hair in a braid and letting if fall over my shoulder - but not anymore, not after last night. Inspecting myself in the mirror, I question who this new woman is.

Sean remained in constant contact with me throughout the day, sending messages and making phone calls. Every time she asked if I'd left the apartment, I'd reassure her that

I hadn't - although part of me wanted to. She sent me pictures of herself at work - overwhelmed by several screens of code and an enormous coffee mug; when she asked for one of me, though, I refused - completely self-conscious about how my body would appear.

You're fucking blind, Kara. I love your body and I'll make sure to show you my favorite spots when I get home.

I look at that text message with wide eyes. Setting my phone on the counter next to the food I ordered, I try to figure out what to do next. The day is still young, presenting me with plenty of hours until sundown. Exploring this enormous apartment seems like a good idea; so, I wander through each room, discovering a breathtaking art studio scattered with painting materials and blank canvases - all covered in dust. It's been collecting here for quite some time. How incredible! I see expensive oil paint that I've always wanted but never had the money for. Could Sean have built this room especially for me?

The painting I made for her mother brought us together- nothing could top that. I don't want to upset her by using these materials without permission though; I'm just trying to pass the time since I promised not to leave. So, I grab a canvas and place it atop one of the easels before snatching up a stool and some oil paints. Sitting down in front of the canvas, thoughts of Sean flood my brain. What should I paint now? Probably nothing that would measure up to her mother's gift.

I flip open the bottles and ready my brushes, then get to work. I close my eyes and take a few deep breaths, preparing to paint what comes to mind. The only thing on my brain is Sean. She told me she loved me. How many days had I wished for her to say those words? I capture what

I feel in my center, just like before, when I painted the portrait that brought her to me. Will this painting help me keep her?

Losing Sean now would destroy me. I'd given up everything to experience a love like this. I love her so much. I'm dazed by a delicate tapping on the entryway of the art studio. I pivot, suddenly, with the paintbrush in my hand. A beautiful lady remains in the passageway wearing an exquisite suit.

"Wow, you are talented." She says as she enters to view the canvas. I stand up, my hands and arms covered in oil paint which is hard to clean off. I set down the brush and move aside as she nears me.

"Are you Abby?" I inquire. She grins at me with her beautiful short curly hair pulled back by a headband, cascading over her shoulders. She holds out a brown bag for me.

"It's still chaos at the office, but Sean made me promise to drop this aftercare package to you. It should have all you need." I flinch, yet accept the sack.

"Thank you." I answer, glancing away.

"Don't be shy," she assures me, "I'm Sean's assistant. I've dealt with far worse. Last night, for example, I drove an irate tarantula to the pet store to be rehomed." I clench my teeth together.

"I'm so sorry about that. I didn't think I'd faint like that." She shrugs nonchalantly, not taking her eyes off the painting.

"After Mrs. Philips passed away, her family got divided—especially on splitting the assets. Sean's siblings hated her since she had majority share of the company. Your painting really helped her get through hard times; she was so adamant on finding you. She fell in love with you even before she knew you. Be gentle with her." I nod as I press a hand onto my chest.

"Looks like she'll probably marry you when she sees this one." I glance at Abby skeptically. Exhaling deeply, she reaches into her purse and grabs a measuring tape.

"Let me get your measurements just in case..." She wraps it around my waistline.

"Don't be silly; she won't—" We both jump due to another knock at the door. Scowling fiercely, Abby looks up at the person standing in the doorway who happens to be Derrica–the woman whom Abby was flirting with during the dinner party. Derrica glares at me hatefully as Abby barks out a question, "How did you even get inside?"

"I'm just collecting my clothes that I left behind," Derrica replies coolly. She turns toward me with her hypnotic brown eyes, making me feel uncomfortable.

"You're just the flavor of the month. She'll tire of you too, just like the rest of us," Derrica sneers maliciously, licking her lips with mischief. She whirls away and strides towards Sean's bedroom, Abby quick on her heels. I brush my hair out of my face and blindly follow them. Her words sting like a knife.

As we enter the room they'd been in together before, it finally hits me: the terrible truth. Not my silly fantasy.

"Get out Derrica," Abby enunciates, furious.

"Does Sean even know you're here?"

Derrica ignores her and rummages through Sean's bottom drawer to find a pair of her panties. She eyes the vacant tank on her dresser wistfully.

"Did Charlotte get out again?" Even she knows Sean's spider? My shame is embarrassing to behold.

Abby shrugs nonchalantly.

"Nope - Sean replaced her with someone else last night.

Kara." Derrica's eyes widen and her jaw slackens in disbelief.

"No way! She loved Charlotte more than anything." Abby merely shrugged again, unaffected by Derrica's reaction.

"Looks like she found something she loves more than her pet tarantula - she's at Garden City Pet Store waiting for someone to take her home if you're interested."

Derrica shook her head grimly, slipping the panties into her pocket before storming out of the apartment without a word.

"Sorry about that - I told her to wait downstairs," Abby apologizes as she starts to leave but I grab her arm tightly to stop her from going anywhere.

"I guess she knew you were up here and got jealous."

"Can you get me out of here? Drive me back to my apartment?" Tears well in my eyes. I just want to escape. It was my mistake. Abby scowls at me.

"No, she'll fire me and likely come after me with vengeance. Why do you need to go? Is it because of Derrica?" I wipe away the tears on my face and stare at the bedroom.

"Is Derrica wrong? We both know Sean is flighty." Abby sighs but doesn't reply. Her nonresponse speaks volumes. She places her hand on my shoulder.

"Don't leave. I understand it's hard, but hang tight until she gets back." I remain behind, watching Abby walk away, pondering if I'm making the right choice.

14

———

Sean

"Fuck!" I slam my fist into the doors of the elevator leading to my apartment. It's not moving fast enough for me. Of course Derrica had to show up then; and that lingerie in my drawer? A clear setup. She was planting traps for the next woman, trying to assert her authority. But I'd been honest with her - it had always been sex. If she ruined the one thing keeping me alive, I will fucking destroy her.

The doors opened to reveal a dark and frigid apartment. No one was here. The lights were out. I quickly moved through each room, heart thudding against my chest until I came across the art space I'd made for her. Turning on the lights, my breath caught at the sight before me: a painting she'd worked on while waiting for me. Tears welled in my eyes and I silently sobbed, unable to lose again...

"Sean?" Kara's voice cut through the darkness from the living room - past midnight, I had been stuck at work most of the day, wanting nothing more than to be with her. So I had worked overtime destroying my mental health to get the server back online, even canceling my meetings just so I could recover and spend more time with Kara... She hurried towards me.

"Oh, my gosh, Sean, what's wrong?" She pats my chest and peers into my tear-stained, pained face. I suppress my sobs, inhaling deeply.

"I thought you'd left me." My reply barely audible above a whisper.

"I considered it. Derrica really upset me. But I promised you that I'd stay and be here when you came back." I press our foreheads together, still breathing heavily.

"I'm so sorry."

"I love you, Sean - that hasn't changed, even with Derrica showing up. But, I'm not sleeping in that bed knowing you slept with her in it." I close my eyes and exhale a sigh of relief.

"You'll have a new bed by tomorrow afternoon." I declare resolutely. She throws her hands up in frustration.

"You're taking me home Sean." I draw her into an embrace; despite her protests, I know she wants to be here with me.

"I will buy us a house if that's what you want Kara - do you understand the power you have over me now?" Momentarily quiet, she places her hand on my chest; she can feel the pounding of my heart against it.

"I'm never sleeping in that bed again." Turning away from me she returns to the couch and lies down, while I remove my shoes and crouch onto the sofa beneath her: picking her up and placing her atop me.

"Sean no, go to bed - you said—" I seal her lips with mine before she can continue protesting any further.

"Wherever you sleep is where I'll sleep for the rest of my

days, Kara." My whisper mingles with hers as we remain connected through our kiss. She sighs and snuggles into the crook of my neck while I close my eyes in gratitude that she stayed with me tonight.

"Derrica was hurt you got rid of Charlotte," she tells me. I laugh at that. Kara lifts her head to look up at me.

"Derrica was scared of her; I said if she didn't like it, she could leave. But you," I say, gripping her shoulders. "But with you, it wasn't a question — I want a future with you." She gasps and I seize the moment for an emotion-filled kiss. My desire to take her to bed is immense, but I'm grounded for the night, so I let her rest against my chest. As she clings to me, I love her more for not abandoning me in this nonsense. Eventually, exhaustion wins and we drift off together on the sofa.

When morning comes, I wake up alone and immediately search for her. I find her in the art room finishing a painting of me and wearing pajamas Abby picked out for her wardrobe. Today, every item has to be unpacked from those bags and put away — she isn't a guest anymore; she's my wife. She smiles when she notices me and sets down her brush. I walk towards her until our lips meet in a sweet morning kiss. She strokes my cheek softly while saying, "Good morning!" Her loving greeting fills me with warmth. Then she turns back to the painting.

"It's beautiful, Kara," I say, captivated by the painting of me on the riverfront; looking peaceful and content. She has a way of seeing me that no one else does.

"Fuck," I growl. Kara looks at me nervously.

"What's wrong?" she queries, her brow furrowing in concern. I'm angry because all I want to do is fuck her – but my bedroom privileges have been revoked. Without another word, I storm out of the art room and grab my cellphone. I dial Abby's number.

"Sean, you said I could have the day off," she reminds me regretfully. This is going to cost me...

"I know," I sigh into the phone. "I'm sorry, but I need a new bed." Abby giggles hysterically on the other end of the line.

"*I REALLY like Kara!* I want a promotion!" I groan in response.

"Fine. Just make sure you get it here before day's end."

"I'll get it done," she replies and hangs up. Exhaling heavily, I enter the bathroom to brush my teeth. Kara joins me shortly after.

"Did you just order a new bed?" she asks, seemingly surprised. Our eyes lock as I state resolutely: "Kara, I'm not going another day without being able to fuck you." Her mouth drops open in shock as a smile tries to claim her lips – turning me on even more.

15

———————

Kara

I sink into the comfy sofa, observing Sean and the movers haul the old bed out of her room. As I sit here in silence, fragments of last night's conversation with Sean's ex-girlfriend flood my mind. Sean thinks I don't understand the the power I hold over her. She got rid of Charlotte because I fainted and agreed to replacing her old bed because I won't agree to sleep in it anymore, and that has me pondering over how much control I have over her. Barely a day has passed since then, yet she's already replacing it with a new one. A smile tugs at my lips as I realize how deeply Sean cares for me.

But as my gaze shifts to the empty space where the bed once was, an urge takes hold of me. To ravish her body like never before, to feel her quiver beneath me until she's screaming my name. Last time it was all about me; now it's her turn to experience that pleasure.

Finally, it arrives - our new bed for making countless unforgettable memories together. Sean walks up to me, planting a kiss on my lips. "What are you smiling about?" she asks.

"You," I reply, watching her slide down next to me on the comfy couch.

Her fingers toy with mine, twirling around my ring finger before I jerk my hand away playfully. But there's something else I want from her first; to make love with her, and only her. Taste every inch of her being until she's crying out with pleasure.

As the movers enter our bedroom to install the new bed, Sean follows them inside. And soon enough, we'll be christening this new bed together in ways that leave us both breathless.

I can't believe she did this for me. As the movers leave, Sean pause to slip some cash in their pockets as a tip, then jump up and rush to the closet to find something sexy. After digging through bags of clothing, I finally spot it - a sheer silk night gown.

When I emerge from the bathroom, Sean is already on the bed, wearing just her sports bra and boxers. We had the same idea! She's transfixed as I walk towards her. Her mouth falls open, taking in my outfit.

"You don't like the dress?" I ask hesitantly. But before I can finish my sentence, she moves into me and grabs my panties, yanking them down. I step out of them and she pulls my night gown over my head. Now, standing before her completely naked, I'm suddenly aware of how exposed I am.

"Don't get me wrong Kara, I love you in these night gowns," she growls hungrily, licking her lips. "But I'm so hungry for your pussy right now, I'd rather you be naked." She dives onto me, burying her face between my legs and inhaling deeply, taking in my scent. I shudder at her touch and back away slightly.

"Grrrr. Come on baby, please." I grin as I hear her pleading. I climb into bed, and she follows suit, mounting atop me. My skin tingles as she takes hold of my breast, kneading them together. A gasp escapes my lips as her mouth latches onto my nipples, suckling both of them.

"Ahhhhh." Pleasure radiates through me as I revel in the sensation. *Stay strong Kara, stay strong.* The core of my being clenches when she does it again; she's about to get me. Taking a deep breath, I grab her arms and lift her up before I lose all strength and self-control. She whines in protest but I act quickly to take control of the situation. Rolling her onto her back, I straddle her form.

"No. I want to try you now," I tell her with an authoritative air. Sean stiffens beneath me as if in anticipation or fear? Only one way to find out. I look up at her face intently,

"Show me what to do." Her expression softens for a moment before shifting back into a gentle smile - understanding my lack of experience - and she guides my hand down to her clit, positioning my fingers against the small nubbin of pleasure that awaited us both. Sean closes her eyes as if ready to surrender herself to this pleasure we shared and moans with delight as I begin to move my fingertips in circles around her clit. As if risen from the depths beneath us, her lip's part and her breathing increases in intensity with every passing moment - like a drumbeat leading us ever closer to the edge of impulsiveness that we found ourselves upon. Unable to take it any longer, I lean down to put my mouth on hers wanting only to taste the pleasure that she emits; joy exploding within me when I feel her body tremble beneath mine - pleasure washing over us until there is nothing else left but satisfaction itself.

"Kara, AHHH!" She gasped, quivering as orgasmic pleasure rushed through her body. I smacked my lips, dying to savor her essence. I freed my hands from her boxers and clasped them firmly around her ankles, pulling them down. She weakly tried to resist me but was too feeble. Sliding down her body, I opened her legs and was dazzled by the sight of her. Her pussy was beauteous.

"Kara, I can't..." Her cries only ignited me more and I kept going even when she told me to stop. Without hesitation, I plunged my face between her legs, burying myself in her sex. Her hands clenched tightly onto the sheets while she arched her back in delight. Every lick sent shuddering waves through her body as I relished the taste of her; sweet like watermelon. I kissed her as if were our first time all over again.

"I love you Kara, I love you." Her chant echoed louder and stronger each time I licked her. My tongue swirled deep into her core, eliciting a pleasurable moan with every nibble. Although she fought against me with every thrust of my tongue, I kept going until I drained her orgasm from her body. But before I could continue devouring her she pulled me up to her with roughness in her grip and crashed her mouth on mine. Our tongues entwined like fingers in a passionate embrace as she tasted herself on me.

16

Kara dominated me. She pleasured my body until I lay in submission. She desired to own me.

Now she does.

I've experienced magnificent sex over the years, scintillating toe-curling sex, but nothing compared to this. Making love. She made me feel so incredible. I felt adored. Unconditional love. She moaned into my mouth when I deepened the kiss. I broke the kiss and trailed kisses down her chest. I clutched her breasts, gathering them together so I could nuzzle her nipples. I adore how it drives her wild. She trembles and comes undone every time I do this. Her eyes shut and she moans, arching her back. I suckled her until she begged for an orgasm. I yearned for her pussy on my tongue. I moved from her chest, back to her lips, kissing her deeply one more time before turning her onto her stomach. She gasped and looked back at me in confusion when I pulled her up onto all fours. I spread her legs apart then forced her face down onto the pillow.

She cried out when I invaded her pussy from behind. She groaned, pushing her ass into me further. Her sex was slick with need. I couldn't resist, swatting her juicy ass and digging my nails into it while devouring her pussy.

"Sean, Mhhhh!" Kara moans as I thrust two fingers deeply into her sex. Grasping the back of her hair, I plow into her. She pants and her ass smacks against me with each forceful stroke.

"AHHHHH! I'M GONNA CUM!" She shrieks relentlessly. Her pussy clamps down hard on my digits, immersing them in her orgasmic relief. Pulling out, I shove my fingers into my mouth, greedily licking them clean before I plunge my face back in her ass and slickly clean her pussy.

"Yes, yes...uh....." She cries out for the second time as she climaxes once again. Her taste is heavenly; I just can't take my mouth off her. At last, I reluctantly pull away for air and pout when she flops onto the bed. No big deal, I'll have her straddling my face later on.

I slide beside her and let my head rest on the pillow. She's flushed from her double-orgasm, a beaming smile plastered on her face as she meets my gaze.

"Can I at least pack up my apartment if I'm moving in here?" She jokes lightly but I give a nod in response to her question. My finger softly traces up and down the bare skin of her back while waiting for her to calm down.

"So now what?" She inquires after resting. "I just move in and be your live-in girlfriend?" Again, I chuckle at her remark. But the truth is: she's not just my girlfriend--she's going to be my wife very soon. Although I say nothing, worry that this may frighten her creeps through me.

"Is that what you want? You want to be my girlfriend?" She narrowed her eyes at me, her frown deepening.

"I don't know," she said, biting her lip. "I just know I don't want to share you." I reached out and gently cupped her face in my hands.

"Tell me, Kara. Tell me what you want from me." Her cheeks flushed as she hesitated.

"It's wishful thinking," she whispered.

"Sometimes wishes come true," I replied softly, my eyes finding hers. "Look at us. We wished to be together, and now we are." Her expression softened into a smile, yet she still seemed hesitant.

"I want...I want to be your wife," she finally mumbled, her voice barely audible. I rolled onto my back and pulled her on top of me, suddenly filled with an overwhelming joy that left me breathless. The thought of having her all to myself was more than enough for me; the fact that she wanted it as much as I did made me feel like the happiest woman alive. As she straddled me, I brought our joined hands to my face and started playing with her ring finger again.

"Do you mean that, Kara?" I asked, needing the confirmation even though I knew the answer already. She bit down hard on her lip and tears began filling her eyes without warning — but they looked happy.

"Yes, Sean," she confirmed with a strained whisper. "Will you marry me?" With one deep passionate kiss, I answered yes without saying a word; when I broke away, she breathed out a shaky question: "Is that a yes?"

"Yes," I declared with certainty as my fingers found their way back inside of her warmth. A wide smile spread across her face while tears streamed down her cheeks.

Time for round three.

Two weeks later

I yank the gate to the storage unit shut and slip the key into my pocket. Kara wants to keep her old furniture for donation. I was about to toss everything, except her art supplies, but that would land me in deep waters if she got angry. We got married within a week of her asking me for my hand. However, it wasn't without argument. She had insisted on keeping her job at the coffee shop—which I detest—but what she doesn't know is that I own the building the coffee shop sits in, making me the landlord.

And she's gonna kill me if she finds out.

My most vital possession resides there for sixteen hours every week. There's no way I won't have control over that building. Kara strolls toward me and takes hold of my hand, giving me a sweet kiss.

"Why are you so glum?" she inquires. My pouting is due to her not letting me ravish her in the truck. I slap her rear and she giggles.

"You can have me when we get home," she breathes out. "I've been moving all day. Let me get a shower first." She slaps my hand away. I like her pussy with a little tang to it. I grin wickedly and bury my face in her neck.

"You're so nasty, Sean. Stop!" She tried pushing me away again. I tugged her back into my embrace. At the moment she was protesting but I wanted what I wanted, and I always get it. Kara had taken to indulging me too much. My hand returned to her butt. I wanted to make her cum with just my fingers, then savor her essence.

She scanned the area for any witnesses before whispering in my ear: "Unlock the storage unit." I gave her cheeky ass one more squeeze before complying, then pushed her inside. Her panties were already off, ready for me to take what I craved.

God, I loved this woman.

17

———————

Kara

Abby trails me from the kitchen into the living room, her hands firmly grasping a large tablet. She scrolls through houses, urging me to pick one to tour. I just moved into this apartment; I don't want to relocate again. But Sean is pressuring me to get a house. A place where we can settle down. I flop down on the couch, savoring a pretzel. Abby holds out the tablet towards me once more.

"Mrs. Phillips, please just look at these." I squint my eyes at her. She knows I detest being addressed that way by her; she's Abby and doesn't need formalities from me.

"Stop calling me that." She rolls her eyes in annoyance.

"You're my boss now... but fine... I'll call you Kara." I smile at her and pilfer the tablet.

"At least select a city for me - I'm weary of Sean hassling me about it all the time. I'd love to work on something else." My request was simple enough.

"Detroit - something within walking distance from the

coffee shop." As soon as I said it, Abby frowned with disapproval.

"What?" I regarded her curiously, contemplating what Sean had done this time around.

I'd already lost it with her when I found out she bought the building that housed my employer, making her my boss's landlord. Now, what had she done this time? She hated the fact that I worked there part-time; it was something to do. Her siblings weren't accepting of our marriage, and that broke my heart—Sean had introduced me as her wife, but they didn't even acknowledge me. They despised her because their mother had blessed her with the majority shares of their company.

She was there now, arguing with them over a new investment; they couldn't move forward without her signature. Since I wasn't involved in their business babbles, I stayed home when not working at the coffee shop.

"What did she do?" I growled at her. Abby groaned.

"She's going to kill me," she muttered, then looked at me pleadingly.

"Sean bought the coffee shop," she said slowly. I gaped at her in disbelief. Oh yes, I was going to kill her; sleeping on the couch for a month wasn't enough punishment. I grumbled madly, hating it when she made these decisions without consulting me first.

"To be fair," Abby squeaked, "it was a good retirement offer she gave your boss—he was having some financial issues and was burned out from owning a small business." Although I was still angry, I couldn't deny that my boss had been extremely stressed lately.

"But that means I don't have a job now," I grumbled. Abby smiled sympathetically.

"She bought the shop for you. You're a coffee shop

owner now." My mouth gapes in shock. Alright, so she won't have to stay on the couch duty for a month. She gets to sleep between my legs for a month. I hand her back the tablet.

"There's one more thing Kara." Uh-oh. I dread whenever she says that. Taking out an envelope from her pocket, she hands it to me.

"This was dropped at the office today. It's from your mother. She tried to get access to Sean, but she was in a meeting." I receive the envelope and scrutinize it carefully. It's definitely stamped with my mom's signature stationary; blue enveloped adorned with motivational stickers. Drawing in a deep breath, I try to find my composure.

I take in a deep breath and ponder about why she would reach out after years of disowning me. After marrying Sean, my name became infamous as the woman that had stolen her off the market—clearly they were well aware of my current financial status. A wave of sadness sweeps over me as I lay eyes on the envelope and wonder why she did so. I brush away the thoughts and set it down on the table before turning towards Abby who offers comfort through her gentle stroking of my arm.

"Sometimes family can be the worst. Don't ask me how I know." I smile at her.

"Well, now that I have a city of choice, I'm looking for houses." Abby stands up with her tablet and strides toward the elevator.

I spend the rest of the day in a trance. The envelope dominates my thoughts; should I open it or keep running from them? Here they come, trying to take away my newfound happiness.

I pass the time making dinner. I'm teaching myself how to make baked macaroni and cheese, attempting to perfect my cheese sauce. Sean walks in afterward, obviously drained from interacting with her family. She's been negotiating with them all day. Despite her exhaustion, she's still gorgeous in her polo and khakis. She rips off her work badge from her belt and throws it on the counter. Her beautiful hair is held back in its usual messy bun, some strands falling against her cheek and neckline. She goes behind the counter to give me a kiss.

"Before you ask baby, my day was terrible. How was yours?" She peers into my pots, curious about what I'm cooking up. I try to act cheerful but fail miserably; Sean notices immediately. Not wanting to burden her, I remain silent about it. But she knows how much worse my family reacted to my coming out than hers.

"What's wrong, baby?" Sean turns off the stove and sits me down on the sofa. She won't give up until she knows what's bothering me.

Her gaze falls to the blue envelope on the coffee table with my name written across it and she picks it up, noting that there's no stamp.

She hands it to me but I throw it back onto the table and she grins. "Well, now we're getting somewhere at least. I know what's got you feeling glum. Now, let's see how I can fix this."

I gape at her in disbelief. "You can't fix this Sean. It has nothing to do with you. You are perfect and you didn't do anything wrong."

Sean licks her lips as if she already knows what the answer is. Oh, God, here we go again—her solution for everything: sex. Lots of sex.

And the sick part is, I freaking love it.

18

———————

Sean

I groan, biting into Kara's neck as she digs her fingers into my back. She cries out in pleasure, cumming for the third time. I love to make her cum. Her pussy clamps down on my fingers; they're drenched with her hot wet sex. I can't wait to lick them clean later.

"Sean!" She screams in my ear. I'll have to feed her later, but right now I have her exactly where I want her. I roll her onto my chest and grab the envelope from the end table. She buries her face in my sweaty chest, moaning softly, not wanting to talk about it. Fuck it. I'm gonna do it myself.

Ripping open the envelope, I pull out a letter—it's from her mother. I gasp and wrap my arms around Kara protectively. It doesn't take long to figure out why she had been so anxious lately – family. I relate too, my own wearing me down today trying to get an agreement from me on a new investment. They'd buy me out if they could, but that isn't happening anytime soon.

"Let's take a vacation," I suggest, squeezing her tightly against me.

"Two weeks... anywhere you want to go."

Kara moans into my chest as she reads the letter—it's polite but bland; her mother wishing her well but not acknowledging our marriage or me at all—but asking to see Kara nonetheless. That's something we both know won't fly —they are ultimate bible thumpers and neither of us wants them influencing what she believes in.

Family—fucking family.

"No, I have a coffee shop to run now," she replies as I shift my gaze away from the letter in my hands to look into her eyes.

"Shit, Abby told you huh?" She nods and moves her mouth towards my body.

"Fuck." A moan escapes me when she spreads my legs. I'm not usually fond of this type of pleasure, but when Kara does it....

"Ahhhh, shit!" I cry out when she wedges her tongue inside me. If her intent was to distract me, then she has won the battle. I cum hard in her mouth as the letter falls away and my hand drops down to her head, pushing against her as the intensity of my orgasm subsides. Grabbing her again by the shoulders, I pull her close for a passionate kiss, savoring the taste of both of us on each other's lips. She quickly pushes the envelope and letter off the bed with one arm while deepening our embrace with the other. We both know there is a conversation that needs to happen; however, neither of us are willing to bring it up at this moment in time. Therefore, I try to avoid any further discussion by rolling her over onto the mattress and playfully fight off giving me another orgasm.

Later that night, I wake with a start, feeling Kara lightly

tapping my arm. Although the sun has yet to rise, it's already very early in the morning. When I focus on her, she's frozen, tears swelling in her eyes.

"Kara?" I worry and then take note of Charlotte on her chest, puncturing her skin with her fangs. Fury boils inside me as I jerk Charlotte off and swing her away so forcefully she hits the wall with a thud like I've tossed a rock. I race for an empty container, locking Charlotte within it. Then I return to Kara who is motionless--naked and wide-eyed-- covered in bites.

"Baby!" I bellowed, scooping her into my arms. Frantically, I searched for my phone and called for an ambulance, followed by security to inquire what the hell was going on. This was clearly an inside job.

I hastily dressed Kara before the paramedics arrived and opened the door for them. Their best efforts were undertaken to treat her, though she needed to be brought to the closest hospital immediately. Grasping her hand in mine, I left with them. Someone had done this to my baby and I had to find out who—Abby knew exactly where Charlotte had been dispatched, so she would have to answer first.

Fortunately, Kara's injuries weren't life-threatening but she'd gone into shock. They kept her overnight for observation and although she was relatively upbeat about it all, I wasn't. She could have been lost forever and that thought made me break down once more as I noted the IV taped to her arm; this was all my fault. Her throat felt dry, so I retrieved the ice water from the tray and offered it to her.

"Sean, stop," she said as I wept again but I couldn't take my own advice. Not until Abby entered nervously after a soft knock on the door. Dressed in her pajamas, clutching her purse and work tablet in hand, she had some serious explaining to do. She gazed at Kara sorrowfully before handing me the tablet."Derrica," she murmured.

"I'm so sorry, Kara," Abby muttered, her remorse spilling from her lips.

"It was my careless words that told Derrica where I took Charlotte for rehoming. I never imagined she'd be so cruel."

Kara sighed, shaking her head."I remember that, Abby. It's not your fault."

"The fuck it's not!" I snarled, my anger radiating throughout the room and making Abby jump in fright. Kara gasped at my intensity.

19

Kara

I'm exhausted, feeling like my body is a furnace, but if I don't calm my wife, I'll lose her. Sean's captivating green eyes are so dark and brimmed with anger, it's as if she was possessed.

"Abby, put the tablet away and go home. We can tackle this after I'm discharged." Sean begins to yell, yet I seize her arm with whatever strength I have left. A cry of pain escapes me when I flinch.

"Ouch!" Sean races to my side, caressing my cheek gently. Her attention shifts completely onto me.

"I'm sorry, baby. My apologies," she murmurs over and over again. I nod for Abby to grab the opportunity to leave, and she does. Sean doesn't look back until the door slams shut behind her.

"Let it go about Abby, Sean," I murmur weakly. She snarls at me in response. "

When Derrica showed up that day, she mentioned Charlotte. It seems like she wanted her released again to hurt me.

Abby defended me and let Derrica know you had gotten rid of her quickly, then related where she had taken Charlotte in reply. Derrica stormed out after that." Sean buries her face in my hair, kissing me repeatedly.

"I should have never adopted Charlotte for a pet. If only I'd known the chaos I would foment..." I shake my head in dismay. All I want now is to fall asleep.

"No Sean. Charlotte is very important to you. Is she alright?"

"I don't know," she mumbled, "and I don't care." I groaned in response. She tilted my head gently and kissed me softly on the lips. Even though Sean was softening, she was still distant. I sighed heavily and let my head slump back onto the bed.

"I need you to try and stay calm for me... Please promise me that much," I whispered weakly. Sean stared at me with glistening eyes, almost as if they were begging me not to ask her for anything more than that.

"Derrica tried to take you away from me; if you're asking me to let go of it, I can't do that. But for now, I can set it aside." Again, I groaned.

"I'll accept that. I want to go home," I murmured. Sean quietly grabbed her phone and started talking to Abby about a new apartment. My little moment of lucidity had passed; my eyelids seemed like they weighed a million pounds, and soon after, I fell asleep.

I awoke the next morning with a cool towel atop my forehead – it was Sean, trying to break my fever.

"Looks like you've made it through the worst of it," she said reassuringly while placing the cloth back on the night-stand. "We can get you home today." She leaned in and gave me a kiss before stepping back and laughing.

"Your breath stinks." We both shared a lighthearted

chuckle before I attempted to sit up, only for her to push me back down into bed.

"I need to pee," I inform her. She emits a resigned sigh and requests the help of a nurse. The attendant soon arrives, they both assist me in standing so I can go to the toilet. Although I want to do this alone, Sean isn't having it—she stands vigil over me as I groan through it. When I'm done, they take me to the sink to wash my hands and give me a care bag with my toothbrush, floss, and other items for hygiene. My eyes drift to the shower.

"Brush your teeth first," she urges, removing her clothes before turning on the shower. She helps me in and washes me from head to toe with exquisite tenderness—making me feel like royalty in her arms. Her attention to detail brings a warmth that spreads through my chest. As she lathers my hair in shampoo, I can't help but vocalize my admiration for her caretaking.

"I'm so grateful I married you," I weep. She grins and kisses me before lowering my head underneath the shower to rinse off the soap. When I step out of the shower, she helps me into something more comfortable and escorts me back to the bed. The nurse had changed the sheets when I returned. Sean appears relieved that she is also freshly cleaned. She has not left my presence. My skin is itching, an ordinary reaction according to the nurse. Charlotte had dispersed her hairs as a protective measure; it will take a week or two for me to heal fully. The nurse informed me that death from a tarantula's bite is rare—for which I am thankful—but Sean refuses to think positively about it. To her, this was an intentional attempt to eliminate me, but only my influence prevented her from revenging.

I'm aware of her ulterior motives though. Her dark eyes are plotting something wicked. It brings to mind how vindictive and cunning she can be at times. I've experienced her brutal side several times already and it was excruciatingly painful. Derrica is in danger and there's nothing I can do for her. Squeezing her hand, I draw her attention away from her gloomy contemplation, eliciting a smile when she sees me.

"Would you like me to get something for you to eat?" Despite being hungry, what I really want is for her to stay with me in my arms. Pulling her off the chair, she climbs up into the bed alongside me.

"I can't wait to get home and just relax; I really hate hospitals." She kissed me, her hand soothingly stroking my back. I looked up at her, pouting my lips for another kiss. Her face lit up with a smile as she obliged me.

"I love you so much, Sean." The kiss this time was deeper, and if she wanted to take it further here, I wouldn't mind. I could use some relief after that scare.

"AHEM." A loud voice disrupted us both, frightening us anew. I glanced over and my horror returned: it was my mother.

FUCK. FUCK. FUCK!

"Mom!" I shouted, jumping to attention. Sean appeared confused but backed away from the bed nonetheless. I scowled in my mother's direction before seizing her hand and pulling her back towards me. Uniting our hands together, I brushed them against my mouth while giving Sean an affectionate look. She thought my mother could change my feelings – not a chance in hell.

~

THE END.....

Stay tuned for part two!

PART TWO SYPNOSIS

Kara:

Someone wants me dead--but I don't know who, or why. They want to keep Sean and I apart, yet she remains the love of my life. I'm trying to savor what we have together in spite of outside forces debating our relationship. My mother has come back into my life berating me for loving a woman--but I refuse to give up on my wife. These tests may be difficult, but I can endure them; losing Sean isn't an option for me.

Sean:

I've been told once or twice that I'm the queen of petty. Maybe that's true. Someone is trying to hurt my wife, and I won't accept that. I just want to be happy with her, but person after person seems to be getting in our way. I'm going to uncover who did this and annihilate them. My only worry at the moment is Kara's mother and her capacity to influence my beloved wife. What she doesn't know is how far I'll go to protect my wife.

ABOUT AUTHOR

Jenna Kent

Jenna Kent, coffee lover, and book lover of all things romance with a sweet spot for masculine dominant femmes resides in Wayne Michigan, just about 20 miles from Detroit, Michigan.

Would you like a free steamy romance book by Jenna Kent? Download here:

https://BookHip.com/VCKVXNH

Check my link in bio for more info!

https://linktr.ee/jennakentbooks

Subscribe to my newsletter!

subscribepage.io/QNoPd8

Instagram @jennakentauthor